PAINTED BLOOM

PRIYANSHU SINHA

"You dreamt of it,

I made it done!"

Contents

Introduction

In life, we often find ourselves chasing after something beautiful, something that promises fulfillment and joy. But, what if the very thing we sought, the thing we believed would bring light into our lives, harbored darkness within it? *Painted Bloom* explores the concept of duality — the contrast between what appears perfect and what is hidden beneath the surface.

This story takes you on a journey through the complexities of love, grief, and the quiet struggles we face in the shadows. It explores transformation — not just the blooming of something new, but the painted petals that conceal the unseen forces shaping our lives. A sunflower, typically a symbol of warmth and light, takes on a deeper meaning here. Its vibrant petals speak of growth, hope, and beauty, while the darker, painted hues beneath suggest that even the most radiant things can be tinged with sorrow and mystery.

Through the protagonist's eyes, we navigate a world where trust is both fragile and precious, where every connection leaves an imprint on the heart, and where the truth is not always as clear as it seems. *Painted Bloom* is a story about the layers of human nature, about the masks we wear, and the hidden truths we either ignore or seek to uncover.

As you turn the pages, you'll be invited to question what it means to truly know someone. Can we see them for who they really are, or do we only see what we want to see? And in the end, when the bloom fades, what remains of the person we once thought we knew?

In the end, *Painted Bloom* reminds us that sometimes, it's not the beauty we should fear, but the painted petals that conceal the deeper truths beneath.

PREFACE

In every bloom, there is beauty, and within every petal lies
a story untold. Painted Bloom is a journey through a world
where nothing is ever as it seems, where love, manipulation,
and loss intertwine to create a narrative that lingers long
after the last page is turned. It is a tale of love that shifts,
of bonds that break, and of a mystery so deeply woven into
the lives of the characters that it remains elusive until the
very end. The protagonist, whose name remains hidden in
the shadows, leads us through a life turned upside down.
At first, the story seems simple—a young person caught
between memories of a friend lost and a new bond that
forms with the enigmatic Zaya. But as the chapters unfold,
the delicate petals of this seemingly innocent connection
begin to unravel, revealing something far darker beneath.
Zaya, a girl who initially seems like a comforting presence,
becomes something far more dangerous, her intentions
twisted by a past that the protagonist is only beginning
to understand. In the course of their relationship, the
protagonist moves through an emotional labyrinth,
struggling with what's real and what's manipulated. The
lines between truth and fiction blur, as what seemed like
a straightforward bond becomes a complex web of deceit,
hidden motives, and haunting memories of those who've
come before. Rashmi and Vikram's deaths—once dismissed
as tragedies—take on new meaning as the protagonist
starts to uncover the dark truths behind their deaths,
linking them to the very figure they've grown closer to. At
its heart, Painted Bloom explores the fragility of human
emotions—the way love can shape and distort, how trust
can be both a weapon and a shield, and how a single person

can alter the course of another's life in ways unseen. It is a story of growth, of awakening to the darker parts of oneself and others, and the struggle to come to terms with the fact that not everything beautiful is pure, and not all that is dark is evil. This book is not simply a tale of mystery; it is a reflection on the complexities of relationships and the secrets that people, consciously or unconsciously, choose to keep hidden. The painted bloom represents something that appears flawless at first but, when peeled back, exposes the raw and sometimes painful truth lying underneath. Each chapter, like a petal, brings us closer to the revelation, and in the end, we are left to question the nature of truth itself. As you step into this world of intertwined lives and blurred realities, I invite you to reflect on the stories that people tell and the truths they bury. Be prepared to question everything you thought you knew about the characters, about the world, and even about the concept of beauty itself. Sometimes, the most profound truths are not the ones we seek, but the ones that find us when we least expect it. May Painted Bloom challenge the way you see the world, and leave you with a lingering thought about the blossoms in your own life, painted in colors both dark and light.

In every bloom, there is beauty, and within every petal lies a story untold. *Painted Bloom* is a journey through a world where nothing is ever as it seems, where love, manipulation, and loss intertwine to create a narrative that lingers long after the last page is turned. It is a tale of love that shifts, of bonds that break, and of a mystery so deeply woven into the lives of the characters that it remains elusive until the very end.

The protagonist, whose name remains hidden in the shadows, leads us through a life turned upside down. At first, the story seems simple—a young person caught between memories of a friend lost and a new bond that forms with the enigmatic Zaya. But as the chapters unfold, the delicate petals of this seemingly innocent connection begin to unravel, revealing something far darker beneath. Zaya, a girl who initially seems like a comforting presence, becomes something far more dangerous, her intentions twisted by a past that the protagonist is only beginning to understand.

In the course of their relationship, the protagonist moves through an emotional labyrinth, struggling with what's real and what's manipulated. The lines between truth and fiction blur, as what seemed like a straightforward bond becomes a complex web of deceit, hidden motives, and haunting memories of those who've come before. Rashmi and Vikram's deaths—once dismissed as tragedies—take on new meaning as the protagonist starts to uncover the dark truths behind their deaths, linking them to the very figure they've grown closer to.

At its heart, *Painted Bloom* explores the fragility of human emotions—the way love can shape and distort, how trust can be both a weapon and a shield, and how a single person can alter the course of another's life in ways unseen. It is a story of growth, of awakening to the darker parts of oneself and others, and the struggle to come to terms with the fact that not everything beautiful is pure, and not all that is dark is evil.

This book is not simply a tale of mystery; it is a reflection on the complexities of relationships and the secrets that people, consciously or unconsciously, choose to keep hidden. The painted bloom represents something that appears flawless at first but, when peeled back, exposes the raw and sometimes painful truth lying underneath. Each chapter, like a petal, brings us closer to the revelation, and in the end, we are left to question the nature of truth itself.

As you step into this world of intertwined lives and blurred realities, I invite you to reflect on the stories that people tell and the truths they bury. Be prepared to question everything you thought you knew about the characters, about the world, and even about the concept of beauty itself. Sometimes, the most profound truths are not the ones we seek, but the ones that find us when we least expect it.

May *Painted Bloom* challenge the way you see the world, and leave you with a lingering thought about the blossoms in your own life, painted in colors both dark and light.

PROLOGUE

The world has a way of painting over the cracks, layering on bright colors to hide the darkness beneath. It's easy to forget that every bloom, however vibrant, was once a seed—tiny, fragile, and full of potential, but also vulnerable to the harsh winds and cold nights that threaten its survival. We all start out like that: innocent, unaware of the forces that will shape us, the people who will enter our lives, and the moments that will forever alter our paths.

For me, it all began with a friendship—a bond so pure, or so I thought, that nothing could ever shatter it. Vikram and Rashmi were my anchors, my connection to a world that seemed safe, predictable. We laughed together, we fought together, and in our youthful minds, we believed nothing could touch us. Until it did.

The first loss was sudden, a crack in the surface that I didn't see coming. Vikram, my best friend, someone who I thought would always be by my side, was gone. No warning. No explanation. Just gone. The weight of his absence was unbearable, and for weeks, I was lost in the dark, trying to piece together what had happened, trying to understand why the world felt colder without him.

But then came Zaya. She appeared as if from nowhere, a presence that seemed to offer comfort in the wake of my grief. She became a distraction, a welcome escape from the pain of the past. But even in the warmth of her company, something felt off. She had a way of pulling me closer, drawing me in, all the while keeping a part of herself hidden in the shadows. A puzzle I couldn't quite solve, and the more I tried to piece it together, the more the pieces slipped from my grasp.

It wasn't until Rashmi's death that everything began to unravel. The truth, it seemed, had been waiting, buried deep beneath the surface, where only the bravest—or the most desperate—could see it. And the more I looked, the clearer it became that the answers I was seeking were not simple, nor were they kind. There were no innocent explanations, no comfort in the truths I found.

The things I learned were terrifying. Zaya, the girl I had trusted, the girl who had filled the emptiness left by Vikram, was not who she seemed. And the deaths of my friends were not the tragic accidents I had believed them to be. They were deliberate, orchestrated, and tied to a darkness I had never imagined.

But what could I do? What could anyone do, when the truth is more twisted than we could ever expect? The bloom, once beautiful, now seemed to wilt under the weight of its own secrets, and I was left standing, alone, amidst the petals, trying to make sense of a world that had become nothing but a tangled mess of lies.

This is my story. It is not one of heroism or glory, but of survival. It is about the lies we tell ourselves, the masks we wear, and the truths that can destroy us if we're not careful enough to uncover them. The world is full of painted blooms, their petals so vivid, so inviting. But behind every bloom, there's a thorn waiting to draw blood.

And if you're not careful, you might just find yourself caught in it.

"मन के बहकावे में ना आ
मन राह भुलाये भ्रहम में डाले,
तू इस मन का दास ना बन,
इस मन को अपना दास बना ले"

"This line is something," I said.

"Means?" Vikram, my friend, asked.

"I mean, this is just normal lyrics, but it says a lot."

"Yes, it does. But do you understand what exactly it says?"

"Don't be deceived by your mind.
The mind loses its way and gets confused.
Don't become a slave to this mind.
Make this mind your slave."

"Hmm... nice translation, but I meant, what exactly does it want to say?"

"Don't be fooled."

"Exactly, don't be fooled..." And then he turned towards Rashmi and smiled at me, giving me a sideways glance.

Rashmi, my crush. We've been in the same class since school, but she's never noticed me. She sits a few benches ahead, and I like it that way — it gives me a chance to watch her without being too obvious. I notice everything about her: the little badge on her bag strap, the Barbie sticker on her notebooks. She's the kind of girl who doesn't wear makeup, always leaves her hair open, and stays in the background and still brightens the most.

In the middle of all the noise and gossip, she's the quiet one. In a room full of people, it's like she's not even there. She always sits in the corner with her small group of three friends. They're close, always helping each other out with whatever problems they have. While the rest of the class rushes through their days, talking loudly and moving in groups, Rashmi remains in her own world — calm, distant, and somehow always out of reach.

"Brother? Are you in your 'sweet dreams' again?" Vikram asked teasingly.

"Ahhhh, shut up, dude. Let's focus more on our topic."

"And the topic is?"

"Well... It was... Trigonometry. We have to practice the questions. The exams are near." I tried to divert the topic, and we started solving the questions.

"By the way, are you ever gonna talk to her?" He asked.

"I'm not sure. Never had such an opportunity."

"We can make one. Wait."

"Vikram, no, wait... WAIT..." I knew I was loud, louder than I needed to be. The eyes turned towards me, and I gave an awkward smile at my classmates.

Vikram didn't stop. He went directly near Rashmi and started talking to the other girl sitting beside her.

"Hi, I heard you were having some problems solving the math. You can ask him," He pointed towards me. "He will help you." And I waved, nervously. At least he didn't go to Rashmi directly, but the girl who sat behind him.

He came back to me.

"What the hell, dude?" My eyes were wide in shock.

"What? Now Rashmi knows that you're good at math. She will come to you to ask questions."

"But the other girls now know too."

"Well, be the honey to attract the bees." He winked.

"What about the lyrics I told you a few minutes ago? I want to focus on my studies."

"By looking at her, smiling when she smiles, getting sad when she gets scolded?" Vikram knows about my feelings towards Rashmi. He noticed me looking at her instead of focusing on the studies.

"Ahhh..."

I started solving my questions. I saw a few feet approaching me. Some girls and boys surrounded me. They all had some mathematical questions. I solved all their doubts. I was looking for a special doubt, a doubt that only she would have, a doubt that only I could solve. Then I started sweating. My heart was pounding fast because then she came. Rashmi placed the math book and pointed towards a question. I had already solved the same question, so I just passed my notebook towards her (I know, I should have explained it to her for better communication, never mind).

Vikram slapped my head. "Stupid"

She walked away with my notebook. I sat there silently. I had given her my notebook in which I was working. I had nothing to do at that time. Then she came again. The air was filled with the smell of roses, her smell. I closed my eyes to focus better on it. It made me happy, it made me smile.

"Hi." She was standing beside me.

The silence broke. She said 'Hi,' she talked to me, her first word to me. I was happy. My eyes started glittering. My face showed happiness. The smile said it all.

"Here, take your notebook. I understood the solution. Thank you." She left the notebook on my desk and left with a smile.

I did not say a word. I sat there while she stood beside me for 10 seconds; I did not respond to her 'hi'. I did not say a word. I did not smile at all. I just kept sweating.

"Dude... She talked to me. We exchanged words." I was flying. But there was a man with ropes who could destroy my hopes, and his name was Vikram.

"Exchanged? She said 'Hi,' and you were just staring at her with a creepy-stupid smile. You should have said something. A word, like 'welcome,' or 'no problem,' or anything. Mr. Genius-Dumb."

"I was nervous."

"You weren't nervous, you were dead. Your whole face is white right now. Are you even alive?" He touched my forehead. "Okay, you're good."

The teacher came in to teach.

We all sat in our respective seats. The class started.

"Might she be thinking how stupid I am? Or maybe, 'What kind of stupid guy is this?' She surely must be thinking that. I should have replied to her, or maybe at least said 'Hi.' I have to be prepared for the next time. What if there is no next time? What if she won't talk to me again?"

"Shut up, dude." Vikram punched me.

"Oops, sorry, was I loud?"

"Oh no, I was just listening to your thoughts."

Among the multiple eyes, I felt a pair fixed on me. I have noticed her for a long time, but never this much. Those eyes were filled with rage. Those eyes were ready to do something, anything. I turned, and the eyes behind the specs turned towards the professor. I knew those eyes were on me.

"I think she…" I turned towards Vikram.

"Shh. This is an important topic. Let's focus there for now."

During lunch, we went to the canteen to eat something. My eyes met Rashmi's. She smiled at me. I smiled at her, too. She came to me and said, "I have one more doubt, may I take your notebook again?"

"Thank you," I said with a shaky voice.

Vikram pinched me from behind.

"I mean, yes, sure you can. Just come to my desk after lunch, and I'll give it to you."

She left with a smile, maybe a small laugh.

"'Thank you?'" Vikram asked.

"Well, let's eat." I lowered my head in embarrassment.

While eating, I felt warmth coming from somewhere. Not physical warmth, but one that made me uncomfortable.

KNOCK- KNOCK.

Someone knocked over the bench behind me. I turned.

"Hi, my name is Zaya. I needed some help with math. Can you please help me?"

"Yes, sure, let me complete my lunch, then we can…" I raised my hand to check the watch.

She grabbed my hand. "Good, let's meet then." She went away with a smile.

There was something in her voice. Her eyes filled with confidence.

I went back to the class. I saw someone had dripped lots of water near my seat.

"Who did that?" I asked.

"Don't know. It was there when we came in. We have asked the janitor to clean this." One of the classmates replied.

I sat in my seat. Vikram was sitting beside me, and he seemed fine. He was looking at Rashmi and teasing me, "Dude, she is looking at you. She is waiting for you to get free." I knew I had to solve Zaya's problem first. I started solving her problems.

Rashmi, on the other side, was looking at me occasionally. She was waiting for me to be free.

After I solved Zaya's doubts, she walked back to her seat. I started feeling normal. Like nothing happened. All the seriousness was gone. My heart started beating normally, and I started breathing normally. There was something about Zaya. While I was helping her with her doubts, I felt that she was looking at me, and her fingertips were on my arms.

"Hi," Her rose smell was in the air, the melody entering my ears. She came, she came to talk to me. Rashmi was near my seat, smiling.

"Sorry for making you wait. Here, take my notebook." I gave her my notebook, and she went back to her seat.

"'Here, take my notebook,'" Vikram mimicked me. "Dude, why didn't you solve her problem here, like you did for Zaya? How dumb can you be?"

I realized my mistake. I turned towards Rashmi to say something, but I stopped. She was walking, and as soon as her feet touched the water on the ground, she slipped and fell on the ground. The notebook fell on the ground. She was on the floor. Her head hit the corner of the bench, and blood was dripping out. Everyone in the class panicked. No one knew what to do. We all stood up and ran to help her. Someone picked up my notebook and left it on my seat.

I turned, and Vikram was looking at Zaya, his eyes were wide in shock. I, then, saw Zaya smile at me.

The teachers were rushing towards our class. The whole floor was echoing with students' screams and cries for help. Rashmi was on the ground, the blood flowing out of her head continuously.

I was stuck there. My eyes were watery, but I noticed something – I noticed a smile, a smile on Zaya's face.

Vikram tapped my shoulder; I knew that touch. He tried to give a signal to me without saying a word. I turned towards Rashmi. The teachers were taking her to the hospital. They carried her and ran to their car. The ambulance was taking a long time, so they decided to take her in their car.

We followed them till the gate. The guards stopped us.

"We will take care of her. You all get back to your classes." One of our teachers ordered us.

We all went back, followed by a few other teachers.

Our English ma'am entered our class.

"Students, I know this is a very tense situation. It's okay, she will be okay. The teachers took her to the nearby hospital. After school is over, you all can visit her. She will feel good." She opened her book. "Okay, I will take the class for now. Let's open your books."

We grabbed our bags and started looking for books and notebooks. I was still thinking about Zaya, and she was smiling. There was something strange about her smile.

Vikram came close to me and said, "It's suspicious how she was smiling at that time. I know she was far from there, but still, her smile indicates that she must have done something, or just maybe she enjoyed that."

I was listening to him, but I wasn't paying attention to what he was saying. My whole attention was on her smile, which was coming to me again and again. There were a few wrinkles over her face caused by the strange smile she was wearing.

"You both." The teacher threw her chalk at us. "What are you both doing?"

Everyone around started laughing at us. I put the book on the desk and started focusing on the subject. The teacher began her chapter.

It was a poem, written by a poet. This was one of the most important chapters. Questions never came from this chapter in the exams, but this time, we were asked to put extra focus on this poem.

The poem goes like:

In shadows deep where whispers blend,
He crafts his words, a gentle mend.
With laughter light and a casual sway,
He bends the hearts that come his way.
A smile, a nod, the dance of chance,
Yet deeper threads weave in his glance.
For every choice, a puppet's thread,
In silence spun, where doubts are fed.

The writer wanted to explain something that I was not aware of. The teacher explained the poem, but she couldn't foreshadow the real meaning behind it. Or maybe, she didn't want to explain it.

"The writer had some special creativity," Vikram said.

"Poems are written by poets, not writers," I explained.

"If you can understand that much, why aren't you helping me through the exams then?" He gave me a look.

"Well, I sit in one corner of the examination hall and you sit in another, how am I supposed to help you?"

"Use your brain! You're a genius, you're a mathematician, use maths and calculate the distance and…"

I closed his mouth with my hand. Classmates sitting beside us were laughing at us.

The teacher noticed us whispering and giggling. She shouted at us.

"You both get out of the class and stand there near the door. Don't you wander off, I'll keep my eyes on you."

We both went outside laughing. We were shameless, like most students are in their student life. While walking out, I turned, she was watching me, her hands on her cheeks, a smile on her lips, Zaya was looking at me.

"I want to talk to you about something," I said to Vikram.

"Yeah, tell me?"

I saw multiple students coming towards us. It was not recess; they were having a game period or something, I think. Many boys and girls were crossing us. Some I knew, and they were laughing at me and Vikram, while a few started murmuring among themselves. I saw a girl whose eyes reminded me of someone. She was someone I was not aware of. I'd never seen her, yet I knew her.

"Zaya?" I said.

Vikram turned towards me and said, "Where's Zaya? She's in the class. Where are you seeing her?"

I turned towards the girl again, but she wasn't there. In the crowd of 40 students, I couldn't see her.

"If you want to see Zaya, just peek in the class; she's sitting inside," Vikram teasingly said.

"Why are you teasing me over girls again? First Rashmi and now Zaya."

I was irritated by his behaviour.

"Why do you smile then? Are you attracted? to her? On her strange, creepy smile? You weirdo," he said.

We both started laughing.

"He is correct. I like Rashmi, but I think a lot about Zaya too. For many months I have been thinking about her. I hope I am not having feelings for her."

Vikram suddenly said. "You've been saying a lot about feelings now."

"What?"

"What?"

"What did you just say?"

"Nothing, I was looking outside."

I thought Vikram said something to me about my feelings; it was like he was reading my mind.

Was the wall breaking? Not sure.

LATER ON...........

Finally, the classes were over. We were allowed to visit Rashmi. It wasn't the teacher's responsibility to take the students to the hospital, but the students were individually responsible.

I saw many girls planning to visit her. Rashmi was a very kind and sweet girl. Everyone in our school loved her; she was one of the most respected students our school ever had.

I saw the girls planning, then Vikram went near them, winked at me, and said something. All of the girls turned towards me, their eyes telling me something. I was scared, not sure what Vikram told them.

Then one of the girls gave a thumbs up, as if she agreed on something.

Vikram came to me dancing, as if he were celebrating something.

"What did you say?" I whispered to him.

"We are going to visit Rashmi with them."

My heart skipped multiple beats. I was scared, I was happy, I was nervous, I wanted to punch him, I wanted to hug him. I was having multiple feelings at the same time. I couldn't understand how to react.

I was worried about her, and I was missing her. When I heard that I was going to see her, I became happy.

We were on the way to the hospital. The girls, me, and Vikram took a bus to reach the hospital. While on the way, I was looking outside, the wind blowing through my hair. Everything seemed fine. There was happiness in my heart and on my face, too, which Vikram was laughing at.

Suddenly, something happened. It all went black. I was sweating, and I couldn't see anything around. I moved my hands around—I could feel I was sitting on something, it was a chair. I was in a room for a moment.

Vikram shook me.

I was on the bus again. I was with all of them.

"What happened?" he asked.

"Nothing, it's like I was dreaming. Might have slept or something."

"Hmm... no worries, we are about to reach."

Vikram seemed a bit serious. I had never seen him like that. His face looked a bit different, like he had shaved his beard, and there were some wrinkles near his eyes.

I looked closely. Something was different.

We reached the hospital. The same floor cleaner smell was all over the place. People were coughing and sneezing. I saw many people lying on the bed, some in wheelchairs. We went to the reception to ask for Rashmi.

One of our teachers was there; he came to guide us to her room.

We entered, and I saw her. She was on the bed under a white bedsheet. Her head was covered with bandages. A small transparent tube was going through her hand, providing her with saline water.

I felt bad for her. We all felt bad for her. The girls went near her and gave her some chocolates. On the other side, Vikram and I were standing and looking at them.

"Were we supposed to buy something for her?" Vikram whispered.

"Seems so," I replied.

Boys, always awkward in emotional situations.

We walked close to Rashmi. We both were thinking very hard about what to say.

She turned to me. She was looking at me with her pure brown eyes. One of the most beautiful eyes she had.

"Hi," she said.

Chapter 2 ends.

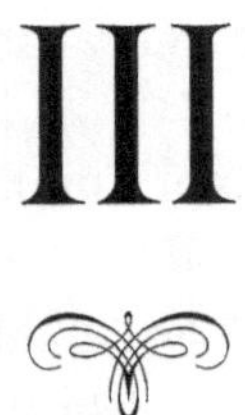

Ever seen ice come out of the refrigerator? The way it melts. I was melting the same way; I was melting on her 'Hi.' It was the most melodious melody.

She was still on the bed, and I was standing in front of her. All the eyes were upon me, waiting for me to reply. Waiting for me to say 'Hi.'

But I stayed there without saying anything. Vikram knocked on my back, signalling me to say something.

"Hi Rashmi, how are you?" I said.

"I am good, how are you?"

My voice was shaking; I was nervous while talking to her. It was not just me and her talking—it was other people's eyes on me.

"I am good too. Your head... is it okay now? Are you feeling dizzy or something?" I asked.

"Umm... no, I am okay. The medicine has taken effect perfectly now, thanks for asking."

I smiled at her, and she smiled too.

Suddenly, everything started turning pink. Someone in the background started playing the violin—melodious violin. There was a rose smell in the air. The cool breeze was soothing my sweat. I was feeling light; it seemed I was floating, it seemed...

"Filmy."

Vikram's voice echoed in my ears.

I turned to him. "What?"

"Well, your conversation." Imitating me, "How are you?" Imitating Rashmi, "I am good. How are you?"

Everyone around started laughing. Vikram was always the funny guy of the class, and his favourite task was to make fun of me.

Rashmi's eyes were sparkling; she was happy from the inside. She loved the fact that her friends came to visit her when she was in need.

"By the way, what happened to you, Rashmi? How did you suddenly...?" one of her friends, Pratibha, asked.

"I am not sure. I was walking to my seat; suddenly, something happened, and I lost my balance. I slipped. The next thing I know is that I was here, on this bed."

We all sat around her. The girls were sitting on the bed Rashmi was on, while Vikram and I sat on the chairs in that room.

Everyone was silent for a few minutes. No one knew what to say. No one knew where to start.

The hospital smell covered the whole atmosphere. The medicine smell, the floor cleaner smell—it was all over. We could hear people crying in the building. Someone must have lost their loved ones. Multiple people were crying, but one of them was louder than the others. Might be a close one. I didn't say anything; I just turned towards Vikram, who was looking out of the window.

His eyes were full of tension. I could see the sweat dripping down from his forehead. I could sense his heartbeat too. He was scared; he was uncomfortable.

"Vikram?" I said.

He turned towards me and placed his hand on my shoulder.

"Let's go," he said.

His voice—there was urgency in it. He wanted to be away from the room, maybe the whole hospital.

"What happened?"

"Let's just move." He turned towards Rashmi and the others. "Umm... actually, we have tuition, and we have a test today. I just remembered. Bye, take care, Rashmi."

He grabbed my hand and pulled me with him. We were running down the stairs. I was losing balance, but he was holding me before I could fall.

"What's the hurry?" I asked him.

He didn't reply. We sat in the cab and left the hospital. He dropped me off first at my home and then asked the driver to drive him home.

"Be careful today. Just meet me at school tomorrow." he said before the cab left.

I went into my room and sat on my bed. I was confused and shocked by Vikram's behaviour. I put my hands in my pockets to remove everything before washing my clothes. I felt wetness near my pocket. I checked my hand—the area around my little finger was red. I checked my pants, and blood was on them.

"Blood?"

I was not sure where it came from. I was not sure if it was mine.

I put my clothes in the washing machine before my mother could find the blood stains on them. I saw my mother; she was watching a series. She likes to watch family drama series and movies while sewing. She was doing the same—sitting on the sofa. On TV, some family drama was playing while she was sewing a new dress.

I ran to my room and closed the door. I opened my books to complete my homework.

While doing maths, I remembered Rashmi came to ask a few questions. I tried solving the questions. I practised them multiple times just to make sure when she comes next time, I don't fumble and solve them like a pro.

"That should impress her."

My mother called me for lunch. I closed my books and went downstairs.

I saw a new vase on our dining table, a beautiful flower blooming proudly in it. I reached out, admiring its delicate petals, but my mother stopped me.

'Careful,' she said. 'This flower came with many thorns. You may cut yourself.'

My mom said.

IV

At the end of the day, I was in my bed. I wanted to sleep but had so much energy—enough to even run a marathon. I didn't know why; I just wanted to be somewhere else instead of lying on my bed.

I stood up and turned on the lights. I wanted to go out and enjoy the night. I wanted to feel the breeze outside. I wanted to feel pleasant. I wanted to feel the coldness in the atmosphere.

I realized something was calling me, something wanted me outside. It was calm; it was the soothing breeze.

I opened the window and sat near it. I closed my eyes to feel the cold air. The air—it felt like someone was touching my face, brushing my hair. I imagined her; I imagined Rashmi sitting near me. It was a childish but pure feeling. I was sad that I wouldn't be able to see her for a few days.

"What are you doing over there?"

I heard my mom walking to my room.

"Close the window and sleep. You have to go to school tomorrow too." She said.

I closed the window and tried to sleep again. I heard her walking away from my room; those loud thumps told me that she was sleepy and angry.

I could still feel the breeze. It was as if those were coming to me directly. Some special presence was there, a coldness—a freezing coldness.

I opened my eyes. It was pitch black. I turned on the night bulb in my room. The AC was off, and only the fan was on, yet I felt cold. I took out my blanket and covered myself in it.

"In the month of September, I'm feeling this cold. How is December going to be?"

I closed my eyes and fell asleep.

I had a dream. A dream of me and someone sitting in a garden. We were sitting together, but we were not together. It seemed she was waiting for someone. I, too, seemed eager to meet someone else.

She—Rashmi—was wearing a yellow frock and golden earrings. She was holding a white petal flower in her hands. I looked around; the garden was full of those flowers.

Someone came. She was happy to see that person. I couldn't see his face as he was hiding it with a mask, but somehow Rashmi knew that person. She went near him and gave him the flower. The other person took the flower in his hand, but withdrew his hand in shock. The flower's stem had some thorns, and the man's fingers were bleeding.

He took out a tissue from his pocket and covered the wound. The atmosphere around us started changing; it was getting denser. I could see his breath coming out of the mask. Rashmi's face started changing. It was someone else's face. I couldn't recognize it, but something was telling me I knew that face.

I started sweating. The flowers around me turned into flames. Everything seemed to be melting. I opened my eyes; I was in my room. The lights had gone out. I was sleeping in a pure hot room, which caused the sweating.

I looked out of the window, the sun was already in the sky.

I got up to get dressed for my classes. I knew that not much knowledge-sharing was going to happen in the classes, as most of the teachers were in the hospital to check on Rashmi.

Our first class was math. As we all know, no matter what happens, math teachers won't take a leave. He was there, in our class. He opened his notebook. He wanted to focus on the chapters, but the murmuring in the class was taking all his attention.

"Okay, class, I know what happened was not something normal. But we need to focus on the class. We need to be prepared for the exam. And to do so, you all are required to pay attention instead of discussing the incident," He said. He was annoyed. The whole school was discussing it—the incident with Rashmi.

He started with Trigonometry. I already knew the formulas. It was just a revision for me, but for the other students, all of them were focused—or maybe they were just trying to be focused.

"Trigonometry is the study of the relationships between the angles and sides of a triangle, especially a right-angled triangle. A right-angled triangle is one where one of the angles measures exactly 90 degrees. In such a triangle, the side opposite the right angle is the hypotenuse, the longest side of the triangle. The other two sides are called the adjacent side (the one next to the angle you're focusing on) and the opposite side (the one across from the angle). Trigonometry revolves around three primary ratios: sine (sin), cosine (cos), and tangent (tan). These ratios are defined as follows: Sine of an angle is the ratio of the length of the opposite side to the hypotenuse. Cosine of an angle is the ratio of the adjacent side to the hypotenuse. The tangent of an angle is the ratio of the opposite side to the adjacent side. These ratios form the foundation of trigonometry, and we use them to solve problems involving heights, distances, and angles."

And the lecture went on. After finishing his class, the teacher gathered his stuff from the bench and looked at us.

"I hope the class was easy. This was just an introduction with some basic formulas. We will start working on sample questions tomorrow. Till then, take care of yourself. Be safe." He went out of the class.

"He seemed pretty serious," Jagir said. He sits behind me.

"Yeah, it's like his mental state was impacted by something," Vikram said.

He and Jagir started laughing.

"Mental state?" Jagir laughed louder this time. I didn't pay much attention to them as I was going through the lesson.

KNOCK KNOCK. Again, the a knocking sound from the desk behind me. The faint rose smell flew in, or so I believed it was the rose smell.

"Hi." Zaya was standing there.

"Oh, hi, Zaya. Tell me?" I replied.

I saw Vikram and Jagir leaving the class.

"I just needed some help with a lesson. I know that you've probably already completed this chapter. Can you help me with it? I'm not that good at Trigo," she said.

"Uh, yeah sure, come sit." I moved a bit, making space for her to sit beside me. I opened the book and went through all the details to help her understand the chapter easily. I looked at her. She was looking at the notebook—no, she wasn't. She was looking at my hand. I snapped.

Her eyes met mine. Everything stopped for a moment. My eyes were watery, and her eyes were confident.

"Umm, guys?" Vikram interrupted. "Are you both done doing whatever you're doing?"

"Uh, yeah, the chapter is over. I hope you understood everything," I turned toward Zaya.

"Yes, of course. I'll try to solve a few questions, and if I get stuck somewhere, I'll call you." Saying that, she left.

"She's gonna call you tonight, buddy," Vikram teased me again.

"Come on!" I shrugged it off.

We then waited for the next teacher to enter and start the lesson. Meanwhile, the whole class was still discussing the incident.

"I saw her falling. She was walking, and then suddenly, she slipped," Jagir said.

"How did she even slip here?" Harsh asked, sitting beside Jagir.

"Someone accidentally left water on the floor, which for sure made the surface slippery. This wasn't an accident. Maybe this was planned for someone else, but Rashmi fell instead."

I turned toward Vikram, who was looking at me. He mouthed, "Zaya?"

We remembered coming into the class and hearing someone say that Zaya accidentally spilled oil and water on the floor. We had no evidence against her, nor were we sure she wanted something like this to happen.

"Maybe it was just an accident," I told myself.

I turned toward Zaya. She was going through the Math lesson, holding a pen in her right hand and a book in her left. She wasn't writing anything, just holding them. Her hand patterns seemed familiar. I knew them, but I just couldn't remember where I'd seen them before.

"What are you looking at?" Vikram asked.

"Ahh, nothing. What's the next class?"

"Hmm, English. No one is coming. Maybe we'll get a free period? Maybe the coach will come in and say in his perfect English, 'Okay students, teacher don't come to school, we play outside. Leave your stuff here in the class and go out and play.' That's what he's gonna say," Vikram mimicked the coach.

The coach came into the class and opened the register to take attendance. Teachers are supposed to take attendance in every class. After the attendance, he checked his watch, looked around at everyone's faces, and said, "Okay students, teacher don't come to school, we play outside. Leave your stuff here in the class and go out and play."

We all started laughing. Vikram's mimicry was on point. The coach looked at us, confused.

We formed a queue and started walking out of the class. We were asked to stand roll-number-wise. It was easy for the first and last persons to stand in their spots, but for the others, it was a headache finding who they were supposed to stand behind.

The queue moved out of the class, and we walked toward the field. I was never good at sports, but Vikram—he was victorious in every game. Name a sport, and he'd ace it. I was jealous of his sportsmanship.

The coach gave us volleyball. Two teams of six boys each were formed. I and a few others were kept as extras.

I turned toward the girls. They were playing Kabaddi. I noticed Zaya and a few other girls sitting on the sidelines, talking. Zaya seemed to be telling them something while the others listened attentively.

V

That evening was like a beautiful dream. The sky was orange and purple, and the cool breeze felt like magic against my face. I could see butterflies all around me, dancing in the air, and the stars were starting to twinkle as if they were joining in on the celebration.

My heart was beating fast, and I could feel every pulse, like my body was alive and flying high. It was overwhelming, in the best way possible.

Then I heard the news—Rashmi had been released from the hospital and would be back in class starting tomorrow.

It was like the universe was telling me everything was going to be okay. Tomorrow was a new beginning, and I was ready for it.

"Are you there?" Vikram asked. He was on a phone call with me. He was telling me what he had heard about Rashmi.

"Yeah, yes, I am here. I was just thinking about something."

"You were thinking about how you're going to hug her when she returns? Are you feeling butterflies in your stomach? Are you looking at the stars and thinking, 'Oh, how beautiful they are, just like my Rashmi,' hmm hmm?

Tell me."

"How suddenly do you start teasing me, Vikram? I was thinking about the maths lecture we had today. I was not thinking about anything else."

"Yeah, sure, you can't hide your blushing face from me. Look at the mirror; is your face red?"

I turned towards the mirror. Indeed, my face had turned red.

"It is red, isn't it?" Vikram was still on the call.

"Yes, because of the sky, which is orange, and the same is getting reflected on our face, making it look reddish. This is simple science."

"Whoa, whoa, nerd. Okay, let's meet tomorrow. Go and grab your pillow, hug it, and sleep hehehe," he said before cutting the call.

I sat at my study table. I opened my books; I wanted to focus on something else. I started playing with my pen. I always play with my pen when I try to focus. I keep the pen rotating between my fingers. I looked at the chapter—trigonometry. I opened my notebook to complete the assignment our teacher had given us. We had some time, about two more days, but I decided to complete it as soon as possible.

The next day.

I was sitting in my seat, hoping to see her. I was expecting a big bandage on her head and that she would enter the class weakly. As she walked, she might feel dizzy again and fall, but I would run to catch her. I would save her from falling and hurting herself again. I would be her hero. And then she would say, "You saved me, my hero," and then she would kiss my cheek.

I was daydreaming when Vikram smacked my head. I came to my senses and realized that Rashmi was already sitting in her seat, and the teacher was already in the class.

I turned towards Rashmi. She looked like a flower—a flower that had lost some of its petals yet was still beautiful. She had recovered from her injuries, but she was still not well. She might need some extra rest.

I was looking at her, and I felt some eyes on me. Those eyes were warm, warm enough to make me feel lazy.

KNOCK KNOCK.

I turned towards the sound. I saw the eyes—they were looking at me. Our eyes met. She was smiling at me, her hands on her cheeks, with some wrinkles around her eyes because of the smile. Her lips were shining red. I was looking at Zaya. I didn't realize it until she signaled me to look at the teacher.

I turned back to the teacher, who had started his lecture.

"During the Indian Rebellion of 1857, several Indian kings played pivotal roles, each contributing uniquely to the uprising against British rule. Bahadur Shah II, the last Mughal Emperor, became the symbolic leader of the rebellion. Despite having little real power, his involvement helped unify various factions under the banner of the Mughal Empire. Bahadur Shah was approached by leaders from different regions who sought his endorsement, thus giving the rebellion a sense of legitimacy. However, after the British recaptured Delhi in September 1857, Bahadur Shah was arrested and exiled to Rangoon, marking the end of Mughal rule in India.

Rani Lakshmibai of Jhansi was another key figure during the rebellion. A widow and the ruler of Jhansi, she was known for her bravery and strategic leadership. Rani Lakshmibai fiercely resisted the British, managing to hold Jhansi against the British forces for several months. Her leadership and courage inspired many rebels throughout the conflict. Unfortunately, after being besieged by British troops, she was defeated at the Battle of Gwalior in June 1858 and died in battle, becoming a symbol of resistance against colonial rule.

Nana Sahib, a key leader among the Maratha nobility, also played a significant role in the rebellion. Initially, he had been granted the title and estates of Bithoor, but the British later dismissed him, refusing to acknowledge his adopted heir. This injustice motivated him to lead the rebellion in his region. Nana Sahib's forces were involved in several battles against the British, most notably in Kanpur. Despite initial successes, his forces were eventually overwhelmed by the British, leading to his eventual flight and disappearance into the surrounding wilderness. The British held Nana Sahib accountable for the atrocities committed during the capture of Kanpur, but he managed to evade capture and continued to be a symbol of resistance for many Indians."

Most of us were sleepy. No one likes long lectures. The teacher understood that we were bored, so he decided to make the class more fun. He asked Jagir to bring other students from the neighboring class. They were students from the 'B' section. They were ahead of us in the history syllabus. The teacher separated the class into two groups. The first group was supposed to act as King A, and the other group as King B. A discussion was going on between us. The topic was 'Who should rule over this land?' The main task was not to start a war but to end this debate with words only.

That was a hard task. The debate was going on, and our teacher was writing something in his notebook.

"Seems like he is marking who all are performing." Vikram said.

We all stated our points one by one. While others were stating their points from my team, I turned around and looked for her. I was looking for Rashmi. She was sitting on her seat silently.

I started looking for another face—the face I was not expecting I would look for. The face with fish eyes, long and thin eyebrows, the face with a gentle yet strange smile, and small wrinkles around the eyes because of the smile. The face whose eyes always stayed on me. I was looking for Zaya's face.

She was sitting in her seat. She was not staring at me; she was not even looking up. She was staring at her notebook. I wanted her to look at me like she did every day, every moment. I wanted our eyes to meet—not romantically, but it felt like I wanted her eyes on me, with her hands on her cheeks and a small smile on her lips.

"Why is she not participating?" I asked Vikram.

"You wanna know?" He turned towards me, placed his hands on my shoulder, and with a smile, he said, "You wanna know, buddy?" His voice was pitched. He was teasing me again.

I hit him with my elbow. He leaned back a bit and started laughing.

The debate was over. So was the class time. All the classes were the same—no serious discussion, just some chit-chat.

The last bell rang. All of us started packing our bags. I turned towards Rashmi; her friends were helping her. I was happy to see her being helped by her friends.

"Bye." A voice came. It was not just a normal voice; the last vowel stayed a bit longer than the other letters. It was the 'bye'; she was trying to let me know she wanted my attention.

Zaya walked past me with a smile on her face, waving her hand.

I said nothing.

I packed my bag and left with Vikram. We were walking down the road, talking and playing. I saw my favorite ice cream shop. I went near it to buy ice cream.

"Kaka, give me this chocolate one and him this mango one," I said while pointing toward the ice creams.

Kaka gave us our ice creams, and we paid him with cash. While walking out, I noticed someone. Someone was standing at the door, but at a bit of a distance. While coming in, I didn't notice her. Zaya was standing there.

I thought she, too, wanted something from here. We walked away.

"She is kinda strange," Vikram said.

"Indeed."

I reached home and started working on my homework.

VI

Another day, another school day. I packed my bag, my mother gave me the lunch box, and then I left for school.

On my way, I met Vikram. It was our mutually decided time to meet while on the way to school. We were discussing the lunch our moms packed for us.

"Good Morning." A voice came. She was standing on the side of the road we were walking on. I turned towards the voice. Zaya. She was standing near the buses on the roadside, just a few paces away from us. She smiled at me. I smiled back at her and increased my pace.

"I got scared; that sudden greeting was scary," I said.

"Indeed. I was not expecting someone to be standing right there and wait."

"We have a strange creep in our class."

"Does she even live around?"

"Not sure."

We both shrugged and continued discussing our lunch.

The class was already filled with students. All of them were early. We sat in our place, and I opened my book. I turned towards Vikram, who was already bursting with laughter, with the other students. He was way too extroverted for someone like me.

I looked around for Rashmi, who was sitting calmly in her seat, reading the books. Her skin seemed smoother than ever. She was fair; her skin was shiny, and her hair was black with a bit of curls at the end. She always looked like a princess.

Someone slapped my head. I turned back. Vikram and a few others were laughing, looking at me.

"What?" I asked.

"Don't look at her like that, dude. Don't be the creepy uncle," Vikram said.

And again, they started laughing. I understood what he wanted to tell me. He wanted to warn me about the girls who noticed me while I was looking at Rashmi. That was bad; no one from her group should know about my crush on her.

I opened my book and continued shuffling through pages. I wanted to distract myself.

Knock Knock.

Everything went silent. I could feel my heartbeat. I turned towards Vikram; his eyes were fixed on someone. I knew who it was. I knew Zaya was behind me. I turned towards her. When our eyes met, a hint of shock was on her face, and then a smile and sparkle in her eyes. A smile that showed her increasing confidence—the confidence of something that she achieved.

"Hi there," She said with the same smile.

"Hi, Zaya. Tell me?"

"I needed your help with Maths. I was not able to solve this question." She handed me her notebook.

I took out my pen and started solving the question while dictating the steps. She was listening.

My heart started racing. A warm sensation spread across my hand—it was Zaya. Her touch was gentle, yet it felt oddly commanding, like an invisible force tethering me to her. I looked up, and she smiled—a smile that was comforting and unnerving all at once.

Then, the teacher entered the classroom, snapping me out of the trance. I stood abruptly, my legs shaky, as Vikram whispered urgently, "Dude, stand up before the teacher notices."

I couldn't shake the strange feeling her touch left behind. It wasn't just a touch—it was as though she had momentarily taken control.

I stood up, still shocked. Zaya walked back to her seat.

"Okay, everyone, let me distribute your exam results," The teacher said. We were all shocked.

"The results are already out? We haven't even given the exams..." Jyotsna said.

All the murmuring turned into silence; all the eyes were focused on her. Everyone's eyes were shocked, and a few laughed. The results were from the mid-semester exam, and she was talking about the final one. Even the teacher seemed disappointed.

"The results are for your mid-semester exam. Now, everyone, I will call all of you to take your results. And, here we have a topper..."

We all knew who it was.

The teacher turned towards me and said, "Want me to take your name? Come and grab it."

I smiled and went to grab the result. I have always been a topper, and then Rashmi was second, and Vikram was third, someone else was fourth, and then Zaya. This was the fixed positioning in every exam result. I was proud of myself; I did a lot of preparation for the exam, and I topped.

The teacher left the class. Vikram and I went out to the washroom. When I came back, I saw Zaya walking away from my seat.

"What was she doing here?" I said.

"Maybe just passing by. Be careful, buddy. The way she suddenly placed her hands on yours, it seemed creepy rather than romantic," Vikram warned me.

I, too, felt some uneasiness when she touched me. Her touch was not normal; it was scary. A sudden spark went through my whole body and told me to look at her. I froze, not knowing what to do.

The school ended. We all packed our bags and were ready to leave the classroom. I saw Rashmi; she was packing her bag. She turned towards me and started walking toward me.

"Congrats yaar," she said. "Always a topper, huh? Let me know your secret. Or maybe, stop studying for a bit so that I can be a topper too." We both started laughing.

"Sure, sure, why not? But for that, I, too, might need something from you," I replied. For some reason, I was confident at that moment. Maybe the results made me confident.

"And what could it be?" she asked.

"A date..." Vikram whispered in my ear and walked away whistling.

I got goosebumps as I realized Rashmi was standing right in front of me—my crush, in all her glory. My hands started shaking like I was holding an invisible jackhammer, and my legs wobbled so much I wondered if I'd accidentally invented a new dance move. My brain screamed, *Say something cool!* but all I managed was an awkward smile that probably made me look like a confused goldfish.

"Umm? You okay? Why are you being Michael Jackson?" she commented on my dancing legs.

"Yeah, I... I am fine," I said. "Well, for your help, can we meet somewhere?" I said, and her expression started changing. "I mean, in the class, I won't be able to help you in any way, as there are multiple classes and disturbances. Maybe after school..."

"Oh yeah, sure, there's a coffee shop nearby; we can meet there after the classes." She stopped for a moment. "By the way, nice save, ha." She smiled.

Vikram came running to me. He grabbed my shoulders and asked, "You asked?"

"I did," I replied.

"And?"

"Tomorrow, coffee shop."

His grip tightened, and his face lit up with a proud smile that mirrored my own. We both erupted with excitement, practically bouncing on our feet. "We did it!" Vikram shouted, throwing his arm around me. We high-fived so hard it stung, laughing like maniacs. He grabbed my notebook and spun it in the air like a trophy while I fist-pumped so enthusiastically I nearly toppled over. If there'd been confetti, we'd have showered in it. The celebration was loud, unrestrained, and unapologetically ours.

The whole class was laughing at us.

Knock Knock.

A smell covered us. It felt like I was somewhere near the rose garden. Rashmi had already left the class, and someone else was wearing the rose. A special presence was there. I felt heavy, as though my heart stopped. I knew who was there; I just knew who was behind me.

"Bye," Zaya walked past me.

VII

It was the day of the date. I was a bundle of nerves and excitement, ready to make an impression. I decided to dress my best, carefully choosing my outfit.

A light blue button-up shirt, left unbuttoned just enough to show a crisp white t-shirt underneath, gave off a laid-back yet stylish vibe. My dark-wash jeans fit just right, striking the perfect balance between casual and sharp. To finish it off, I slid into my clean white sneakers—they were simple but screamed effort.

I checked myself in the mirror, running a hand through my hair for the tenth time. "Not bad," I muttered, trying to calm the butterflies in my stomach.

"Whom are you meeting, Raja Beta?" My mother playfully asked.

"No one, Mom, just going for group study," I said. There was a smile on my face. I glanced at my reflection—I was blushing.

"Uh-huh. Who is coming to the study?"

"Vikram..."

"And..."

"Rashmi."

"And who is Rashmi, beta?" Her tone was more playful now.

"She is a friend." I was trying my best to save myself.

"A friend, huh? Maybe that 'friend' likes the expensive perfume you're wearing. Maybe she likes the colors you're wearing. And maybe she's going to like you, too."

My mom was teasing me. No matter how hard I tried, I knew she understood what I felt for Rashmi. She wasn't just teasing; she was *teasing*.

I grabbed my bag and left home. There was a smile on my lips and a blush on my face. My mother stayed at the door and waved at me.

"Come back soon and tell me the whole story." She said.

I started walking. I was so deep in my thoughts that I wasn't paying attention to my surroundings. I just walked, smiling. Everyone was looking at me, some even laughing, but I didn't care—I just kept walking with a smile.

"Good morning."

Someone greeted me—I didn't notice who it was, whether a boy or a girl. Their voice faded into the background as I walked past them, completely lost in my own world. A comforting warmth wrapped around me, like an invisible hug, and a soft, special scent lingered in the air. But I didn't stop. I didn't look back. I ignored it all and just kept walking, my focus fixed ahead.

I was excited, nervous, and everything all at once. It felt like my brain had turned into a blender, mixing every possible emotion at full speed. Excitement bubbled inside me like a bottle of soda someone had shaken too much, while nervousness weighed me down like a bag of bricks tied to my feet.

My pace was completely out of control. One moment, I was walking so fast I could've given Usain Bolt a run for his money, and the next, I was slower than a tortoise on vacation. At one point, I even tried to run, but it felt so ridiculous that I stopped and pretended to fix my hair. I must've looked like a cartoon character figuring out how legs work for the first time.

My heart was thumping so hard it felt like a drum solo in a rock concert, and my palms were so sweaty I could've slipped off a monkey bar. Every step closer to Rashmi felt like both the best and the worst idea ever. What if I said something dumb? What if I tripped over my own feet? What if she laughed at me? My mind was throwing all sorts of wild scenarios at me, each one more ridiculous than the last.

Still, despite all that, I couldn't help but smile. Rashmi was waiting for me. And no matter how much my nerves screamed at me to run and hide, I knew I had to keep going.

The cafe was in sight, and so was she—my princess.

Rashmi stood near the entrance, wearing a yellow top that seemed to glow brighter than the morning sun. Her golden earrings dangled softly, catching the light every time she moved. Her hair was open, flowing freely with the gentle breeze, dancing as if even the wind itself was trying to compliment her beauty.

Her face had a natural shine, a kind of glow that no makeup could ever create. Her eyes sparkled like the clearest stars in the night sky, and her smile—oh, her smile—was so warm it felt like the world around her didn't matter anymore. It wasn't just her beauty; it was the way she carried herself, like she belonged in a fairytale, and everything else was just background noise.

Even angels would've paused to admire her, realizing they had nothing on the grace and charm she carried. My heart skipped a beat, and I just stood there for a moment, completely lost in the sight of her. She wasn't just beautiful; she was magic.

"Hi." She said. She stood there, waiting for me to reply.

I was out of words. I froze, seeing her like that. My whole body was shaking again, but I had to say something. I had to.

"Hi, Rashmi. Looking good," I said. "Looking good? Seriously, dude? You could've said something else, but *looking good?*" I started scolding myself.

"Well, thanks for that. You look good too. I like your look—full-on hero look, huh?" She playfully punched my arm.

I opened the door for her, as a gentleman should. I pulled out the chair for her.

"Hmm, so do you want something?" She asked.

"No, it's fine," I replied. "I should be the one asking her these things. I should be the one hosting our date. What is going on?" I muttered to myself.

"So, my dear topper. Let's start our study?"

For some reason, I wasn't nervous anymore. It felt like she knew I had a crush on her, and now she was just playing. It felt like I didn't have to be scared anymore, like it didn't have to be a secret anymore.

It seemed easy. It seemed fulfilling. Her smile told me everything. I gathered all my courage and asked her: "I'd trade my recess snacks just to see you smile every day. Will you let me?"

"Finally, after practicing all night, I said it! I didn't stop midway; I didn't mispronounce anything. I did well. I said it perfectly." I was celebrating in my mind. I forgot that she had to reply—I forgot she was sitting in front of me.

"How long did it take you to practice this?" she asked, looking at me.

I was still celebrating in my mind. Her words brought me back to my senses. "What did she ask?" I asked myself.

I turned toward her. She was holding a glass of water near her lips. The water touched her lips, and her brown eyes were fixed on me. She seemed serious.

"Seems like the wrong time." I thought to myself. I had to reply to her.

"It was just spontaneous. I didn't mean anything; it was just..." I tried to cover myself again.

"Again with the cover, huh? I know you like me. I've noticed you looking at me. At the hospital, I knew you would come to see me. Not sure why, but it seemed like you would. You should've said this earlier and in an easier way. Just a normal 'I love you' would've worked, you know?" She tilted her head slightly to the left and smiled again.

I couldn't believe what I just heard. My whole face turned red. I was nervous and excited at the same time. "Rashmi confessed—she said yes?" I couldn't stop myself from smiling hard. I wanted to celebrate with everyone. I wanted to pay for everyone's order. I wanted to give everyone a treat.

"I'm glad you told me this. I was prepared for your proposal."

My celebration stopped midway, my smile faded, and I looked up at her. She was going through the menu. "Someone told her about my feelings?" I couldn't understand what she meant. "No one else knew about this except me and Vikram—at least, not a girl. No one knew we were going to meet. Who told her that?" I was trying to figure it out.

Then I remembered—someone on the way greeted me. "Who could it have been? I'm not sure if it was a he or a she. I remember the smell, it was of roses."

I was still processing everything. I wanted to understand who it was. I wanted to understand who knew about our date.

"What are you thinking?" She asked.

"Ah, nothing. Let's order something and start studying," I said.

She smiled and then ordered sandwiches for both of us. While she was focused on the books, I was thinking about that strange person. I noticed something through the window—someone was there. There was a girl. I couldn't see her face, but she was holding an umbrella and wearing a red dress. I wanted to go out and stop her, but before I could even move, she was gone.

After two hours of our date-cum-study, we both decided to pack our bags and continue studying the next day.

I was happy to spend so much time with her. She seemed happy too.

"Let's meet at school, then." She said.

"Yes, sure." I replied.

She turned and started walking. I wanted to stop her, but I couldn't.

I started walking home. My mother was watching Netflix when I entered the house. I went near her and sat down. She looked at me and smiled.

"How was it?" she asked.

"Yeah, it was good. We discussed a lot of things," I replied.

"Only discussed? Didn't you tell her something?" she playfully asked.

"I did..." Before I could complete my sentence, something happened. A sound reached our ears. We both were surprised.

The doorbell rang.

"Who is it?" I looked at my watch—we weren't expecting anyone.

I went to check the door.

KNOCK KNOCK.

VIII

Milkman came, steel mug juggled in his hand. I picked up the mug and walked towards the kitchen.

I don't know why, but I thought Zaya was outside that door. My heart was beating weirdly. It was not fast; it was not slow. I wasn't feeling excited. I wasn't feeling nervous. It was all nothing. My feelings were blank, my heartbeat was strange, but my brain was blank.

He handed me the milk can and left the house.

"Were you expecting her?" My mom asked as she came from her room.

"Zaya..."

"Rashmi..."

We both said at the same time.

"Huh? Who is Zaya?" My mom asked.

I turned towards her. Her V-shaped eyebrows were pointing towards her nose. Her eyes looked serious, and her face was confused.

"Uh... I meant Rashmi. I mean, no one. I wasn't expecting anyone. I knew this was the time for the milkman. Why would I expect anyone else?" I started looking at the ground.

I heard giggling. I saw my mother laughing at me.

"It's fine, son. This is a new experience for you. No need to be shy." She patted my head and left.

I smiled too and went into the kitchen to boil the milk.

• 42 •

IX

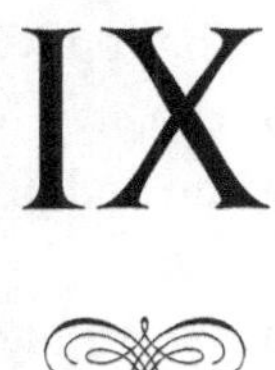

A few days later.

I packed my bag and left for school. I took the same route again, as usual. There were two paths to school. One was shorter, and this one was longer. I always liked this route—I don't know why. There were many houses along the way, all vacant. The route was once inhabited, but now no one lives here.

"Good morning."

I turned. Someone was standing there. She was wearing the same school uniform as mine, holding an umbrella in her left hand and a bag on her right shoulder. I couldn't see her face.

I stopped. I thought of replying, but before I could, she started walking away. She was fast enough to make me run after her to catch up. She unfolded the umbrella. I recognized her face—it was Zaya.

"What are you doing here?" I asked.

"I was just passing by. I live nearby," She replied.

She was giving me a cold vibe. Her tone was calm, and she wasn't wearing any expression. She turned towards me.

"Aren't you getting late for school?" she asked.

I checked the time on my watch. I was on time.

"No, I'm on time. But today, you'll also be on time. Every day, you've been late for class." I tried to be funny.

"No, I'll be late again." She replied.

I remembered that for the past few weeks, she had been greeting me at the same time and place, but always arriving late to class.

We came to a crossroads. We had to go straight, but she took a left turn.

"Where are you going?" I asked.

She didn't reply. She just turned towards me, smiled, and kept moving forward.

I was curious. I wanted to know where she was going. This was the first time I was this close to Zaya. Indeed, she sat beside me during class, but we never had this long of a conversation. I started walking behind her. She knew.

She increased her pace; she wanted to get rid of me. I, too, started walking faster. I was breathing heavily. My muscles were tired. But she—she was walking at that speed like it was nothing for her.

I looked around. Sometimes the area felt familiar, but other times it seemed like another world. I stopped. I was tired. I decided to walk back on my original path to school, leaving her.

I turned back, I started to walk, but I tripped. Something was under my foot. But I didn't feel. Someone grabbed me. It was Zaya. She grabbed me by my arms and tried to save me from falling down.

"Thank you." I said. I was so close to her, I could smell a faint rose fragrance coming from her shirt.

I checked my watch. There were about five minutes left before class started. I panicked. I knew I was late. Even if I started running, I would still be late for class. I turned towards Zaya; she was walking away, and she was a bit far from me. She turned towards me, smiled, and pointed at a building. I came closer to her.

It was our school. It was the backside of the school, a place I had never been. She had made me walk all the way around to the back of the school.

"But why?" I asked her. "Why did you make me walk this much just to get to the back of the school?" I was angry. My breathing was warmer, and my eyes grew bigger in frustration.

"I never asked you to follow me. You came." She said. "Now, follow me. I'll let you into the school before class starts."

I followed her. I entered the class. The whole class was looking at me. The girls were staring—some with anger in their eyes, others with surprise. The boys were shocked.

Vikram mouthed, "What did you do, bro?"

I turned towards Rashmi. Her eyes were red. They were teary.

X

Zaya went and sat in her seat. Her face showed confidence, like she had won something.

I sat down next to Vikram, who still looked shocked.

"What happened?" I asked him.

He turned to me.

"You were with Zaya?"

"Yeah... It's a long story. Actually, I was..."

"Stop, buddy. You don't need to explain to me. But you need to explain to her." He pointed at Rashmi.

Rashmi was sitting with her back straight, staring at the board. There was nothing written on it. After all these days of knowing her, I could tell she was upset. She was angry. Something had happened in just a few minutes while I was walking to school.

"What exactly happened?" I asked Vikram again.

"Someone saw you walking with Zaya. You two were holding hands, and she grabbed your arm. Someone saw it and told everyone in the class."

"That's not true! I was falling, and she saved me from getting my clothes dirty."

"It doesn't matter, buddy. The way people heard it, the rumor made it sound like you and Zaya were having a romantic moment."

"Who spread this rumor?"

"Someone from another class saw you two."

"Someone was following us? I didn't notice anyone else. How long were they following us, and why? How did they even know I was with Zaya?" My mind raced with questions as I tried to figure it out.

I looked around. Everyone in the class was staring at me. They were whispering, talking about me. Some looked shocked, and others looked angry.

I could feel it. The negative energy in the room was directed at me.

The teacher walked in, holding a rolled-up piece of paper. Everyone turned their attention to him.

"Okay, class, we have the final exam timetable. Let me write it on the board." He said.

He started writing, and we all copied it down. This time, there were no gaps between exams. We all knew this would be tough, and many of us might fail. We had four months to prepare.

When the bell rang, the teacher left. Everyone started talking about the exams. I got up and walked toward Rashmi. She was still sitting in the same position as before. Like she was expecting me to give her some explanation.

Her friends, sitting around her, gave me strange looks. I knew what they were thinking, but I didn't know how to explain myself to them. All I wanted was to clear things up with Rashmi.

"Rashmi." I called her.

She turned away, not even looking at me. I knelt down next to her and tried to hold her hand.

She pulled her hand away.

"She doesn't want to talk to you. You should leave." One of her friends said.

"I'm not talking to you. I'm talking to her," I replied angrily. My tone was harsh, and everyone could feel it. I was frustrated. Everyone thought wrong about me, and I only cared about clearing things up with Rashmi.

Her friends stepped back, leaving Rashmi alone. I tried my best to explain what had really happened, but she wouldn't listen. Frustrated, I left her seat and walked out of the class. Vikram followed me.

"Who spread the rumor?" I asked him.

"Well, according to Jaspreet, it was a girl from another class."

"Let's go talk to her," I said firmly.

Vikram stopped. "What are you going to do? She's just a girl. Don't make it worse."

"It's already bad, Vikram. She saw something and spread lies about it. She made everything worse. Take me to her."

We walked quickly toward the other class. I wanted answers. I wanted to confront the girl who had spread these rumors.

"By the way, why is Zaya so calm?" Vikram asked.

"No one is blaming her. Why would she be upset?"

"No, I mean, she's just sitting there, watching everyone react. Her so-called friends are treating her like a hero, and she's smiling."

We stopped. Vikram's words caught my attention. He was correct. She was acting so relaxed, as if she wasn't involved in any of this.

"Tell me more," I said.

"Since you two were together, people should be asking her too. But they're only blaming you. And why did you follow her in the first place? Why did someone suddenly notice you today? How did someone even know you were with her?"

I thought back to the morning. "When I left home, I saw her a little while later. It felt like she was waiting for me. I don't know why, but I followed her. She led me to the back of the school. That's where I tripped, and she helped me."

"Back of the school? Why would anyone walk for that long? Don't you think it's strange? Could be a setup."

"How is it a setup?"

"Why was she near your house? Does she always wait there?"

"Every day, I see her at the same spot around the same time."

"That's suspicious."

"I think so too."

We reached the classroom where the girl who spread the rumor was. Vikram pointed her out.

"There she is," he said.

She was a pretty girl with big eyes. Her slender arms and fair skin made her look innocent. But when she saw me, she smiled.

"I was expecting you." She said.

"Why did you spread the rumor? What you saw wasn't the truth. And how do you even know my name?" I asked her.

"I know everything about you. Your name, your address, your daily schedule, your current partner, and even who your next partner will be."

Vikram frowned. "How do you know all this?"

"She told me." The girl said.

Everything froze. My mind raced. *Who is 'she'?* Was it Zaya? Rashmi? Someone else?

"Who are you talking about?" I asked.

"Zaya." She replied and smiled.

Vikram and I exchanged a look. We both had suspected Zaya, but hearing her name confirmed it.

I ran back to my class. Zaya's eyes were teary as if she had been crying. Instead of confronting her directly, I approached her carefully, wanting to ask why she had done this.

"Everyone is talking bad about me," Zaya said, starting to cry again. Her friends surrounded her, comforting her.

"It's okay, Zaya. We know this is just a rumor. We know you did nothing. It must be him who started this." One of her friends said, pointing at me.

They were blaming me. I couldn't say a word. I started to believe that Zaya might be a victim too. But why was I the only one being blamed?

"Zaya, that girl who spread the rumor, said you told her to do so." Vikram said.

"She was with him the whole time! How could she have spread it? It must be your friend who started the rumor." One of Zaya's friends said defensively.

I stayed quiet, unsure of what to say. I turned to Rashmi. She was sitting silently. I went to her.

"Rashmi." I called softly.

"Don't say my name," she said angrily. "You don't need to explain anything. You were having a good time with Zaya while I was waiting for you. Do you even remember what today is?"

I didn't. Then it hit me. It was her birthday. Her first birthday since we got together. I should have been more careful. I should have gotten her a gift.

"Rashmi, listen. I know I forgot your birthday, and I was wrong. But please, just listen to me—"

"It ends here." She said, cutting me off.

She got up and walked out of the class, leaving me behind.

XI

It had been a few weeks since our relationship ended. We were both avoiding each other, and she seemed unwell.

"Have you both talked to each other recently?" Vikram asked me.

"No. She doesn't even want to see my face. She's avoiding me."

"No worries. It's just a school crush. In the future, you'll get someone better," Vikram tried to calm me.

My eyes were teary. I felt weak.

"This is not manly. I feel weak for some reason," I said.

"Manly? Bro, we're still in school. We're teens. Hormone imbalance is something you shouldn't ignore. It's normal. Be calm and focus on your future," he said.

For the first time, Vikram sounded serious. He made a good point, and I agreed with him.

I turned toward Zaya. She was sitting in her seat, smiling at me. Her lips were shining—she must have applied lip balm or something.

"Are you staring at Zaya?" Vikram asked.

"Uh, no, no. I was just thinking about something."

I sat in my seat with Vikram beside me. The class started, and the teachers were sharing the most important topics for the exams. The final exam—I had to perform better than everyone else.

I made a planned timetable for my studies and prepared it on the back page of my English notebook. I wanted to be at the top again.

"Buddy, show them. Show her that you're a topper." Vikram said.

This was unnecessary, but he said it anyway. I wasn't sure how to take it, but since Vikram said that, I decided to take it positively.

I felt something—something from Vikram. I couldn't connect the dots, but something was off about him. I didn't mention anything.

I turned toward Rashmi. She was writing something. She must have been planning her timetable too. Now, this was a competition between her and me. We were partners, good friends, but for some reason, she had started seeing me as her rival. It was good for her.

"At least she's thinking about me." I thought.

After class, I reached home. I changed my clothes and sat on my bed. I took out my books and started studying according to the timetable. My mother came into my room.

"Have some snacks," she said, giving me a plate of noodles.

While eating noodles, I was going through my math textbook and solving important questions. They were quite easy to solve. But I wasn't properly focusing on my studies. My mind was still revolving around Rashmi. I was thinking about her, just like every day. Whenever I opened my books, I thought about her—her sitting straight, tears in her eyes, and anger on her face.

She was no longer the Rashmi everyone liked. She seemed more serious now, more alone. Her friends were no longer with her. Something had happened in the past few months. Rashmi's behavior had changed a lot. I saw her screaming. I saw her scolding a lot of her friends. I saw her sitting alone during lunch. She was isolating herself, avoiding everyone around her. Now, she only had three friends.

"That's strange." I said to myself.

I took out the last page of my notebook and started drawing lines.

Rashmi used to have a small group of close friends. She was everyone's favorite. She had almost 14 girls as friends sitting around, and now she had only one. Meanwhile, Zaya used to be alone, and now she had 11 girls around her. Somehow, the other girls who used to be Rashmi's friends started ignoring her and were now around Zaya.

"She somehow managed to make the other girls her followers and leave Rashmi. But what did those other girls want before? Why did they switch sides?" I wondered.

I called Vikram and shared my observations. He was shocked too. He wasn't sure if I was just making things up or if this was an actual fact. He had never noticed anything like this.

"Let's discuss it in class. Now focus on your studies," he said.

Like I felt earlier, he wasn't acting like the old Vikram anymore. He wasn't excited about small things. He was serious now. He wasn't showing special interest in anything.

"Something's off with him too." I thought.

The next day.

I went near Rashmi directly. I ignored everyone around. I ignored her friends who were badmouthing me. I grabbed her hand and pulled her out of the class.

"What's going on with you?" I asked her.

"Huh?"

"Why are you behaving like that?"

"What do you mean?"

"You are being alone. Multiple girls are avoiding you now. Your flowery vibe is lost. What is happening?"

"Why are you worrying? Aren't you enjoying your time with her?"

"There is no HER, Rashmi. It was you since the start and..."

She raised her hand in front of my face.

"You don't have to say anything about that. Just say what you wanted to say."

"Your friends, they are not with you. They are being someone's followers. Why is it? And also your behavior, you are being rude now. I saw you screaming. Why?"

She turned towards me, her eyes were red—not metaphorically, but really.

"You don't have to worry about anything. Whatever is happening, is happening for good. Focus on your studies, try to be on top, and let me live my life without interfering." She left.

I stood there. Shocked. My legs were frozen. I couldn't move, I couldn't speak. I was shocked by her reaction. I was expecting her to react like that, but she did more than I was expecting. I came into the class with a blank expression. I wanted to hide what happened out there from others.

But her expressions were easily readable. Everyone understood something had happened between me and her.

My eyes were teary, and I saw her going away. I felt all the eyes falling on me, and I saw a smile among the confused faces. Everything was blurry to me; I was not sure who smiled and who badmouthed me.

"Now what did you do?" Vikram asked.

"I did nothing. We were just talking."

"Talking about?"

"She is being weird and all."

"I told you not to focus on those things. Told you to ignore her. Focus on the book, buddy."

He grabbed my arms and started shaking me. It seemed he wanted me to be awake, but I was awake.

The teacher came and started the class. While Rashmi was giving the blue vibe, I felt a red vibe coming towards me. Not sure where it was coming from. I tried to focus on the blackboard and ignored everything around.

After some hours, the class ended. We all grabbed our bags like usual. I turned towards Vikram.

"Let's try that new ice cream from Sharma's shop. I saw it while coming here," I said.

"Uh, no, sorry. I have some work. I will be going the other way again." He replied.

It had been a few weeks since he started going alone instead of going with me. He started using the longer route, avoiding the path I use. Even while coming to school, I saw him coming to the gate from the other side of our usual path.

"Not sure what's wrong with him." I thought.

He walked out of the class. I was slowly walking behind him. I wanted to ask him where he was going. I couldn't gather the courage for the same. I saw Rashmi coming towards me. I smiled, hoping that she was going to talk to me about something. About anything.

She walked past me. She ignored my existence.

She took a left turn from the gate—the same turn he took.

"Please don't be it." I thought to myself.

I prayed for it to be just my imagination and not true. I never wanted it to be true.

"I am just imagining it. I am just imagining it."

I took the left turn. I wanted to confirm that what I was imagining was just imagination and not a fact.

I saw Rashmi. I was following her. I stealthily increased my pace. She took another path covered with trees. The leaves and branches of the trees were hiding the road. Only half of the path was visible. I somehow saw her; she was grabbing something.

I looked closer. She was holding a hand. There was a smile on her face, and there was happiness. She was with Vikram. My nightmare came true. They were together. I didn't know how to react. My best friend and the girl I love were together.

"I should be angry. Should I just confront them? Should I jump in front of them? What should I do?" I sat on the road, watching them with tears in my eyes.

Someone patted my back. It was Zaya.

"Calm down. It's just human nature to get attracted to someone when in need." She said.

I did not understand what she meant. She then wiped my tears and had me lean my head on her shoulder. I still remember her rose fragrance.

I went back to my house. I closed my door from inside and started crying. I was not sure why I was crying—was it for the betrayal from my best friend? Or knowing the fact that she was now someone else's?

My mother felt my blueness. She started knocking on my door.

"What happened, son?" she asked.

I did not reply. I wanted to be alone. I wanted to be away from everyone. This was the worst nightmare. This was something that I never wanted to happen. Everything was happening in front of my eyes, and yet I was not able to see it. Her ignoring me, him avoiding me. They both used to smile at each other. I never saw anything in their smile.

"I want to kill both of them." I screamed.

XIII

I didn't attend school for a few days. I ignored all the calls from my school. I locked myself in and was coming out only for food. Everyone called me except Rashmi and Vikram. I could see all my friends' names in the call logs, but not theirs.

"Maybe they don't care."

"Why aren't you going to school?" My mother asked.

"Nothing."

"Tell me." She grabbed my hand.

"I am just preparing for the exam," I said.

"Are you telling the truth? Just the exam?"

"Yes, mother."

I went into my room, closed the door behind me, and sat on my bed again, staring at the ceiling. I was thinking about my life; I was still going through a lot. Also, I knew I was not ready for the exam. I knew I was going to fail the exam.

The mobile phone started ringing again. I knew some of my friends might be calling me. I ignored it and continued thinking about my life and my future. I looked toward my book. I wanted to open it and start working on it. I wanted to be the topper again. I wanted to show them all.

I went to my study table. I opened my books. But the phone started ringing again, and it was ringing continuously. I wanted to scream at the caller. I grabbed my phone and accepted the call.

"Hello?" I started.

"Where are you? The police are asking for you." Someone on the other side said.

"Police? Why?"

"Vikram and Rashmi have been found dead."

There was pin-drop silence between both of us. The lights in my room flickered, casting strange, shifting shadows on the walls. My heart began to race, each beat feeling louder in the quiet room. The silence was heavy, almost like it had a weight pressing down on me. It felt as if the air around me had thickened, making it hard to breathe. My hands trembled as I gripped the phone, trying to make sense of what I had just heard. The quiet wasn't just silence—it was unsettling, like something was watching me, waiting. I wanted to say something, but the words wouldn't come out. It was as if the silence had stolen my voice.

XIV

A childish voice asked, "What happened to them? Who killed them?"

The storyteller turned towards the child, who was sitting in front of him with his small mouth open in shock.

The storyteller looked around. He was surrounded by children, all around 5 years old. All of them were shocked. They placed their hands on their mouths, and a few kept their hands on their ears to avoid hearing anything further. But one of them was still curious. He wanted to know more while the others begged the storyteller to stop.

"Do you all want to know more?" The storyteller asked in his senile voice.

The children started running around the room, shouting. The old storyteller began laughing.

"I think that's enough for today. Let's continue tomorrow." He said.

The children sat on the floor, their big eyes fixed on the stout storyteller.

"Okay, it's bedtime. Let's go, kids." The parents said as they entered the room to take their children.

The children grabbed their mothers' and fathers' hands and began walking out the door.

"I have a question." One of the children said. He let go of his mother's hand and sat near the storyteller.

"Who is Zaya?" he asked.

Everyone froze. All the children let go of their parents' hands and sat near the storyteller.

"Is she still alive?" the boy asked again.

"Yes." The storyteller replied.

"Where is she?" all the children asked.

The smile on the storyteller's face faded. His expression turned emotionless, but his eyes showed sadness. He slowly lifted his finger.

"There." He said.

The group of children turned in the direction he was pointing. An old lady sat on the couch, her thin lips curved into a tight smile. Her sharp features and unblinking gaze gave her a stern, almost eerie look. The dim light tangled with her white, messy hair, casting shadows that made her presence feel unsettlingly intense.

XV

The children gathered around the storyteller once again, eager for answers. They wanted to know who killed Vikram, who killed Rashmi, and what more had happened in the storyteller's life.

Meanwhile, their parents weren't pleased with the story.

"He used to tell them stories from the Mahabharata and Ramayana, and now he's telling them this nonsense about deaths and all?" The parents complained.

"Don't worry, let him finish. It's just a story. After this, he'll probably go back to moral-based tales." Someone reassured.

The story continued.

I went to school. The police were there, waiting for me.

"Why haven't you been attending school?" The officer asked.

"I was preparing for the exams. The final term starts next month." I replied.

"Hmm, okay. As you know, your friends committed suicide," he said.

"Suicide?" I asked in shock. "They both committed suicide?"

"Yes. The signs all point in that direction. We also found a suicide note near their bodies," he said.

I was stunned. Just the other day, I'd seen them holding hands, and now they were both gone, apparently by their own will.

"How did they die, if I may ask?" I hesitated.

"Why do you want to know?" The officer questioned.

"Nothing, just…" I trailed off, realizing it was better not to ask more.

"You have to attend class daily. We'll be monitoring everyone," he said before leaving.

Our whole class was instructed to attend regularly until further notice.

The next day.

I grabbed my bag and started walking the same path as usual. My heart was heavy, mourning Vikram. His chatter, his nonsense facts—everything about him was gone.

"Good morning."

Something felt odd. Zaya was still there, greeting me midway as usual. I could see the spot having her shoe prints now. She has been waiting for me there for so many weeks, even the roads recognised her.

She continued walking toward school, taking her usual path. I ignored her and kept walking on my route.

When I entered the classroom, all eyes were on me. Everyone stared at me with pity in their eyes. Their expressions said, *"Poor guy."* Not only had I lost my best friend, but also my crush on the same day, at the same time. But a few still cursed me for cheating on Rashmi. Zaya followed me into the class, and the atmosphere changed with gasps.

I sat in my seat, alone. I needed someone to talk to, someone to fill the void. I looked around but couldn't find a single face to replace Vikram's. There was no smile like Rashmi's, no presence that could bring back Vikram's aura.

I sat silently, staring at the blackboard.

KNOCK. KNOCK.

I knew who it was.

"Zaya." I murmured.

"Yes, it's Zaya." She replied.

Her voice was sweet, confident, and polite. I was surrounded by a rose fragrance—sweet and calming—that made me feel dizzy. I wanted to sleep; it felt peaceful.

"May I sit here?" she asked, pointing to the seat beside me.

"Yes, sure." I said, unsure why. Maybe because I needed someone with me. I was emotionally weak, and she came to give me a hand.

I just wanted that scent to stay. For some reason, I liked her confidence, and for some reason, I wanted her presence near me. I was feeling alone, and she was offering me the hand I needed, ready to hold it.

"Maybe I was wrong about you," I said.

From that day, she started sitting beside me. She became my lunchmate, and unknowingly, she became my friend.

XVI

It wasn't long before Zaya became a part of my life. We started going to school together and returning home as well. We spent most of our time together.

But somewhere in my mind, I was still thinking about Vikram and Rashmi. I wanted to know why they had committed suicide. However, I had a distraction now—I had Zaya. The girl whose name was always last in attendance but who had become the first priority in my life. There was no one for me before her.

"Dinner time." My mom called out.

I went downstairs. My mother had prepared my favorite dish: puri, kheer, and matar sabzi. I loved it the most. I sat at the dining table and started eating. It tasted like heaven.

"So, when are you going to introduce me to her?" My mother asked.

"Who?" I asked, still chewing my food.

"Z-A-Y-A," she said.

I choked on my food. She handed me a glass of water and started laughing.

"Why are you blushing, my son?" she teased. "Don't worry. Just finish college, get a job, and then you can marry anyone you want."

"Ma, don't tease me while I'm eating. And Zaya—she's just a friend."

"Just a friend? Are you sure?" She said, poking my arm.

My cheeks turned red. I couldn't believe how fast I had moved on from Rashmi and forgotten Vikram. The sadness that once consumed me had faded, replaced by the calmness Zaya brought. She was the warmth I needed in the cold void left by their absence.

Unintentionally, I started depending on her presence. If she didn't greet me in the morning, I'd feel irritable all day. Even when she sat beside me in class, she had a habit of knocking on the bench before speaking, and I found myself waiting for that knock.

That night, I lay in bed, eagerly waiting for the next day. I couldn't wait to see her again. I felt excited, as usual.

THE NEXT DAY

Before school started, officers were already in our classroom. They seemed to be sharing some information with the students. I took my seat and waited for them to speak.

"So, students, as you all know, your friends committed suicide. We're here to ask some questions." One officer announced.

"Why now, after so long?" Our teacher asked.

"Because we've found something strange about the case. It was reopened recently, and we discovered some unsettling details."

"What did you find?" the students asked.

"Initially, we thought Vikram died of suffocation, but we found no marks on his body to suggest he strangled himself. However, he did suffocate." The officer explained.

"Was his body dragged there?" Jigyashu, a classmate, asked.

"No, he died there. It was agonizing. We found something unusual in his mouth—sweets. Large particles of sweets, in fact. This attracted red ants, which we found inside his mouth. Some ants had entered his food and windpipe, biting him internally. His throat swelled up, and he suffocated."

"That's dark." Jigyashu said.

"But the real question is how he got there and how those ants ended up in his body." The officer said.

The classroom fell silent. Some students exchanged fearful glances. A few of them looked at me.

"You and Vikram were having some issues, right?" Vinayak said to me.

"That was nothing—a small misunderstanding. What are you implying?" I replied.

"Nothing. Just that you had an argument, and now he's dead in a horrible way. Oh, and your ex, she's dead too." Vinayak added.

I ignored him and turned toward the officer, who was quietly observing us.

"What about Rashmi?" Niti asked.

"She died in a different, equally disturbing way. We found her feet burned. Initially, we suspected it wasn't a suicide, but there was a note. Her legs were covered in burn marks up to her knees. It appears she was electrocuted while standing in water. The room she was found in had a wet floor, and we suspect she died from electrocution." the officer explained.

The entire class went silent, terrified. I instinctively grabbed Zaya's hand out of fear. Her hand felt as cold as ice. When I turned to her, expecting her to look just as scared as everyone else, I noticed a faint smile on her face. It was not visible clearly, but I knew she smiled.

Something didn't feel right. Her reaction to the officer's announcements wasn't normal. I tightened my grip on her hand. She turned toward me, her expression now mimicking the fear of everyone else.

I felt uneasy. There was something about Zaya that wasn't adding up.

"I think I need to keep an eye on her." I thought.

I was starting to feel uneasy about Zaya. Something about her didn't feel right, and I couldn't shake the suspicion that she might be connected to what happened to Vikram and Rashmi. But I had no proof, no way to piece it all together. Even worse, it felt like she knew I was suspicious of her.

Her behavior began to change. She was trying harder than ever to stay close to me. She would pull me away if I talked to someone else, making sure I spent all my time with her.

I didn't know how to deal with it. I started avoiding her, leaving the house earlier than usual and taking a longer route to school just to make sure she wouldn't see me. For a few days, this plan worked, but she began giving me cold, sharp looks in class.

After school, she would always try to walk with me, clinging to my arm and making it harder for me to keep my distance. I became careful not to let her find out where I lived, worried she might start waiting for me outside my house.

No matter how much I tried to avoid her, Zaya kept finding ways to stay close. The more I pulled away, the more determined she seemed to hold on. It felt suffocating, but I couldn't figure out what to do.

One morning, she was not in the class. I thought she was going to be late, but she did not even attend any class. She was absent from school that day. I thought she was ill or something, that's why she didn't come. Happy with one day's freedom, I went home dancing. I rang the doorbell.

My mother was standing in front of me, her face was scared.

"Welcome back." She said.

Her tone was different. She was different, her walk, her body language, everything told me that something was wrong. I entered the room, I saw Zaya was sitting in our drawing room. She smiled at me. I saw there were some photographs on the table.

I couldn't have good eyes on them as my mother pushed me away.

"Go and change your clothes, WE CAN DISCUSS THEN." She said. She was loud in the last part for some reason.

I went into my room. I was scared. I was feeling uneasy. I changed my clothes and went downstairs.

I saw Zaya sitting with my mother. They were both discussing something. I could sense my mother being scared and Zaya being confident and dominating.

I sat near them. I saw the pictures, they were of a wedding ceremony. I looked closely, and the people in the pictures were random; there were multiple themes in the pictures. I was not sure what she was doing with those pictures.

I turned towards my mother, and she just gave me an awkward smile.

"What are these pictures?" I asked Zaya.

"Oh. These are for a wedding."

"Wedding? Whose wedding?" I asked her.

She just smiled at me. The same confident smile, the scary smile. "Ours." she said.

I was not sure how to react, I confusedly turned towards my mother, who was just sitting there with the same scared smile on her face.

"What do you mean Zaya?" I asked Zaya again.

"Don't worry. It's just a marriage, nothing to worry about." She said. This time, her tone was scary. She was being dominated.

She put her hand on my hand and said.

"Don't worry, just follow whatever I am saying, and no one will end up like Vikram."

I was shocked, and I froze in my place. I saw her standing up and leaving the house.

"I will come again, and this time, with my family. You guys just need to say yes and that's all." She said and left our house smiling.

There was silence, an eerie silence. Only my mother and I were left in the house. We were not sure what to do, how to react.

My mother just placed her hand over my shoulder and said, "We don't have a choice. Just follow whatever she is saying."

"But... We can complain to the police about her. She can' just barge in and make us obey her." I said.

"Listen, I wanted to tell you this earlier, but I thought it might seem playful, so I didn't," my mom said with a small sigh. "She's been coming to our house for the past few days. Back when you were going to school every day, just before you came home, she would appear with roses in her hand and give them to me."

"I thought she was just trying to impress me... and she was. Honestly, I was impressed," she continued, a hint of wonder in her voice.

"She would bring chocolates with the roses, sometimes little letters too. I used to think they were meant for you, but she would always say they were for me."

Her eyes softened as she spoke. "She always smelled like roses… that scent, the way she smiled, the little gestures she made… everything about her felt so thoughtful. It's no wonder I was drawn to her. She had a way of making herself unforgettable."

"Mom…" I opened my mouth to say something.

"But… after a while," she paused, frowning slightly, "I started feeling… uneasy. I found myself waiting for her. I would wait for a knock on the door, even though we had a doorbell. And when she came, it wasn't just to give me things. Somehow, she always left with something too—my time, my attention… even my thoughts. It was subtle, almost unnoticeable, but I could feel it. She had a way of slipping in and out of my day, making me feel needed, making me look forward to her visits. It was… strange, but I couldn't help it."

She cupped my cheeks, her hands trembling. "We need to run away from here… or we'll be bound to follow her."

"Run where? You work here, I have my school here. Where can we even run?" I asked, panic rising in my chest.

She shook her head, her eyes wide and serious. "You don't understand… she's not just a girl who comes with roses and chocolates. She's… she's dangerous in her own way. She has a way of getting inside your head, inside your heart. You won't even notice it happening until it's too late."

I tried to speak, but no words came out. Her fear… it was contagious.

"I can't let her touch your life like that," she whispered, gripping my shoulders. "I thought I could handle her, but… she's clever. Too clever. She's already taken more from me than I realized, and I won't let her do the same to you."

She stood up suddenly, her face pale but determined. "I can't stay here. I have to leave... for now. You need to be careful. Watch her, and don't let her in. Whatever she wants, don't give it to her. Not even a little."

Before I could ask anything, she slipped out the door, leaving the room silent except for the echo of her warning. My heart pounded. Zaya wasn't just charming... she was dangerous. And now, it felt like the real threat had begun.

XVIII

"So, you and your mother were threatened by Zaya?" A child asked the storyteller.

"Yes. I'm still stuck with her. I'm old now, and I don't have to worry about much, but I can't do anything. I'm just stuck," he said.

The parents turned toward the old lady sitting in the corner. She was smiling calmly. She stood up, looking more fit than the storyteller. She even seemed younger than him.

"What is your name?" She asked the storyteller.

The storyteller had no answer.

"What's your age?" She asked again.

He couldn't answer that either.

"As you all can see, he doesn't remember anything. He's just making things up, just for the story. Don't take anything serious." She said.

"Yes, aunty, I thought so too. I was wondering why he is not taking his name in the story. Seems it's just a normal story." A child's mother added.

"Yes, hahaha," the old lady laughed.

Everyone turned toward the storyteller. He was looking down, visibly scared. The old lady walked over to him and placed her hand on his shoulder.

"Now he'll say I'm threatening him just by putting my hand on his shoulder." The old lady said, looking at him mockingly.

"That day, when she came to our home, she put her hand on my shoulder and told me she'd kill us. After that, whenever I tried to find a way out of her, she'd threaten me by doing the same thing—placing her hand on my shoulder. She scares me. She threatens me." The old man said, his voice trembling but serious.

"See? I told you!" The old lady laughed again.

Everyone in the room started laughing—except for the children. They believed their storyteller. He had never lied to them before, so why would he now?

"You know, when we were young, he used to say I was a manipulator, like I controlled him." she said, still laughing. "But I'd say, he's the actual manipulator."

The room fell silent. Everyone exchanged confused glances.

"I mean, just look around. At first, he told you stories about mythologies, fictional tales, and moral lessons. He gained your trust. And now? Now he's telling you this story to turn you all against me."

"But why would he want to get rid of you?" A parent asked.

"Oh, it's nothing. He's just suffering from **schizophreniform disorder**. Sometimes, he can't tell if his dreams are real or not. He can't distinguish between reality and imagination. Right now, he believes I manipulated him." The old lady explained.

The parents seemed convinced. The old storyteller did seem frail and often exhibited symptoms of mental illness. Some days, he was terrified, and on others, he was inexplicably angry. The parents looked at the storyteller with pity—he was just a "poor old man."

"So the whole story is fake?" Another child asked.

"Not all the story. The incidents were real, Vikram and Rashmi were real, but me being the main villain was not." She said and every adult in the room laughed again.

"Can you tell us your story?"

"My story?"

"How did you meet him? Who were Vikram and Rashmi? I liked the story. I just want to know more." A childish voice came.

"Sure beta, one day I will."

"Alright, let's end this story here. From tomorrow, Uncle will tell you all a new story. Now it's bedtime." One of the parents said.

The parents started picking up their children and heading home. The children cheerfully left with their families, all except one.

Aryan, a four-year-old, was very close to the storyteller. He believed the old man's version—that the old lady was the bad person and the storyteller was the good guy. He tried to convince his parents to stay longer, but his protests weren't enough to sway them. They grabbed him and led him toward the door.

As Aryan was leaving, he turned back to look at the storyteller. The old man seemed scared, his eyes pleading for help. Aryan couldn't do anything. Feeling sleepy, he closed his eyes.

Then he heard a sound.

KNOCK. KNOCK.

Aryan opened his eyes. The storyteller looked calm, there was no fear in him. He saw the old lady—Zaya—placing her hand on the storyteller's shoulder and smiling at him.

ETA:1857

The year was 1857, a time when India was teetering on the edge of a monumental uprising. The air was thick with tension, the ground beneath trembling with the whispers of rebellion. The British Empire, seemingly invincible, was about to face a challenge that would shake its foundations.

But amidst the chaos of mutiny and bloodshed, a story unfolded—one not chronicled in any history book. Madhav, an ordinary man with an extraordinary device, stood at the intersection of past and present. A wristband, gifted to him by fate, held the power to transcend time. With it, Madhav dared to rewrite the history of his beloved nation, to tilt the scales in favor of freedom. But time, as he would soon learn, is a delicate thread, and meddling with its weave comes at a grave cost.

In his quest to liberate India, Madhav found himself battling not just the British, but the very fabric of reality. Every leap through time unraveled a new consequence—some foreseen, others devastatingly unexpected. His actions, though noble in intent, began to carve out a legacy of chaos, mistrust, and loss.

As Madhav waged his war across centuries, his closest friend, Anant, faced battles of his own. Accused of being an accomplice in Madhav's sudden disappearance, Anant became ensnared in a web of suspicion and fear. With the British authorities closing in and his family in turmoil, Anant's life was forever changed by his friend's daring gamble with time.

This is not just a story of rebellion; it's a story of choices and their far-reaching consequences. It's a tale of how the past, no matter how firmly we believe it is set, can be as malleable as clay in the hands of those daring enough to reshape it. But the question remains—at what cost?

ETA: 1857 invites you to journey through time, to witness the birth of a legacy both mysterious and monumental. In the end, you may find yourself asking: If you could change history, would you? And if you did, how far would you go to live with the consequences?

She Lives In Paragraphs

Some stories don't begin with a plot twist.
They begin in silence.

The kind of silence that fills a room long after the sound has stopped—the kind that presses against the windows, settles into the pages of unopened books, and makes every click of the keyboard feel louder than it should.

That was the kind of silence Priyanshu lived in.

He didn't plan to write this story. Not this kind. Not about love. Not about feelings.

But sometimes, it only takes one unknown email, one strange suggestion, one fleeting thought—
"Try a different genre."

He had written of monsters before. Of shadows and screams and people who never made it to the last page.

This time, he created someone who did. A girl.
With eyes he could never draw the same way twice.
With a smile that changed the rhythm of his heartbeat.
With a name that sounded like poetry.

Kavya.

She wasn't supposed to be real. She wasn't supposed to mean this much.

But day by day, line by line—
She started living, not just in the paragraphs,
but between them.

And the writer, who never wrote for love,
started writing for her.

This isn't a love story.
This is a writer's confession.
Of how a girl stepped out of fiction,
and stayed.

"YOU ARE NEW FOR ME?
I AM RIGEL FOR YOU"

KNOW THE AUTHOR

PRIYANSHU SUNIL SINHA

Priyanshu Sinha is a passionate storyteller, celebrated for his ability to explore complex emotions, historical landscapes, and the supernatural. He is the author of five acclaimed works—Mixed, Mythological Error, ETA: 1857, Painted Bloom, and She Lives in Paragraphs—each showcasing his talent for weaving intricate narratives that stay with readers long after the last page.

* 9 7 9 8 8 9 7 7 7 7 9 8 3 *